SCIENCE EXPLORERS

THE WORLD OF TECHNOLOGY

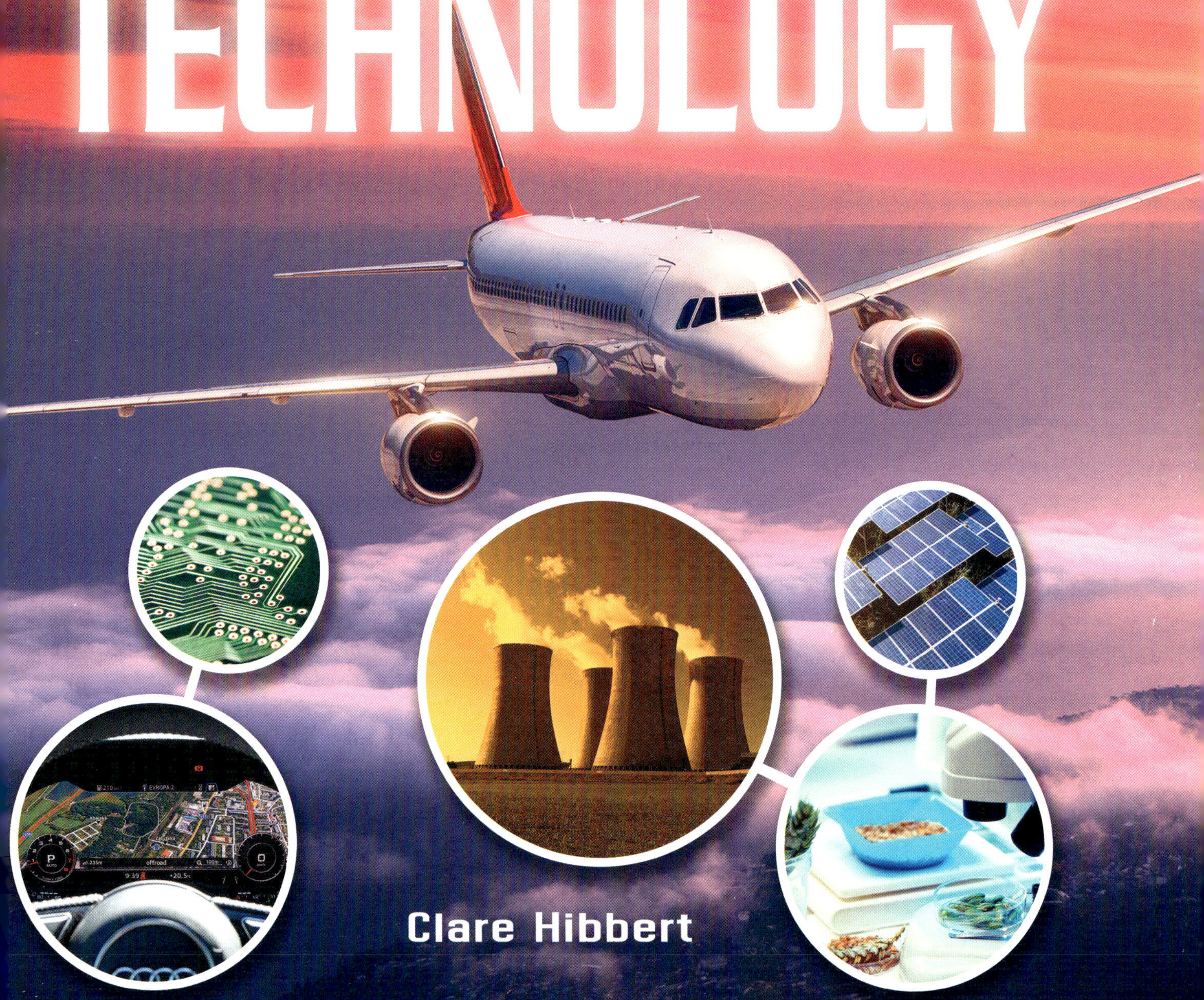

Clare Hibbert

Enslow Publishing
101 W. 23rd Street
Suite 240
New York, NY 10011
USA

Fitchburg Public Library
5530 Lacy Road
Fitchburg, WI 53711

Published in 2019 by Enslow Publishing, LLC.
101 W. 23rd Street, Suite 240, New York, NY 10011

Copyright © Arcturus Holdings Ltd 2019

All rights reserved

No part of this book may be reproduced by any means without the written permission of the publisher.

Cataloging-in-Publication Data

Names: Hibbert, Clare.
Title: The world of technology / Clare Hibbert.
Description: New York : Enslow Publishing, 2019. | Series: Science explorers | Includes glossary and index.
Identifiers: ISBN 9781978506749 (pbk.) | ISBN 9781978506473 (library bound) | ISBN 9781978506794 (6pack) | ISBN 9781978506541 (ebook)
Subjects: LCSH: Technology—Juvenile literature.
Classification: LCC T48.H625 2019 | DDC 600—dc23

Printed in the United States of America

To Our Readers: We have done our best to make sure all website addresses in this book were active and appropriate when we went to press. However, the author and the publisher have no control over and assume no liability for the material available on those websites or on any websites they may link to. Any comments or suggestions can be sent by email to customerservice@enslow.com.

Photo Credits:
Every attempt has been made to clear copyright. Should there be any inadvertent omission, please apply to the publisher for rectification.
Key: b-bottom, t-top, c-center, l-left, r-right
ESA: 14–15; Lawrence Livermore National Laboratory: 20–21; NASA Images: 18cl; Science Photo Library: 4–5 (Photo Insolite Realite), 6b (Universal History Archive/UIG), 10–11 (David Parker), 12–13 (Samuel Ashfield), 12cl (US Army), 16tr (Dr Gary Settles), 18–19 & 27tr (Pascal Goetgheluck), 22–23 (Nicolle R Fuller), 22cr (Philippe Plailly), 24cr (Equinox Graphics), 24br (Gusto Images); Shutterstock: cover main (Denis Belitsky), cover tl (Dario Lo Presti), cover bl & 11br (tomas devera photo), cover tl & 19tr & 32br (Thongsuk Atiwannakul), cover c & 20c (Martin Lisner), cover br & 25tl (science photo), 4tr (adriaticfoto), 4c (Neal Pritchard Media), 4br (YC_Chee), 5tr (adike), 5br (NASA Images), 6–7 (Maryna Kulchytska), 6tr (SherSS), 7bl (NPavelN), 8–9 (mekcar), 8bl & 26tl (Photomontage), 9cr (andrea crisante), 10c (fotografos), 10bl (Luisa Fumi),13tr (Volodymyr Krasyuk), 14bl (Chris Singshinsuk), 15cr & 26br & 31br (asharkyu), 15bl (Blan-k), 16–17 (satit_srihin), 16bl (Peppy Graphics), 17bl (Gabor Miklos), 18bl (AF studio), 20bl & 27cl (Blue Ring Media), 21bl (udaix), 22tr & 30br (Forance), 22bl (Shmitt Maria), 24–25 (Marcin Balcerzak), 25bl (Pogorelova Olga), 26tr (Temnaya_Diva), 26cr (Chim), 26bl (Denys Prykhodov), 27tl (Carlos Yudica), 27br (Anant Kasetsinsombut), 27bl (McGraw), 28cr (Spasta), 29tr (Oleksiy Mark), 29br (aapsky); Wikimedia Commons: 9tl (www.jedliktarsasag.hu), 12bl (Science Museum, London/Mrjohncummings).

CONTENTS

Introduction 4
Simple Machines 6
Engines, Motors, and Generators 8
Electronics 10
Computers 12
Connected World 14
Flying Machines 16
Smart Materials 18
Nuclear Energy 20
Nanotechnology 22
Genetic Engineering 24
Fun Facts 26
Your Questions Answered 28
Glossary 30
Further Information 31
Index 32

Introduction

Science is amazing! It shapes our understanding of the universe and has transformed our everyday lives. At its heart, science is a way of collecting facts, developing ideas to explain those facts, and making predictions we can test.

Laboratory Learning

Chemistry investigates materials, from solids, liquids, and gases to the tiny atoms that make up everything. By understanding the rules behind how different kinds of matter behave, we can create new chemicals and materials with amazing properties.

Scientists can observe chemical reactions under a microscope.

Secrets of the Universe

Physics is the scientific study of energy, forces, mechanics, and waves. Energy includes heat, light, and electricity. Physics also looks at the structure of atoms and the workings of the universe. Even the galaxies obey the laws of physics!

Many forms of energy are involved in a storm.

Chimpanzees are one of around 7.8 million species of living animals.

Life on Earth

Natural history is the study of living things—the countless plants, animals, and other creatures that inhabit Earth now or which existed in the past. It studies how these organisms are influenced by each other and their environment. It also looks at the complex process of evolution—gradual change from one generation to the next.

Electron microscopes let biologists study creatures such as this headlouse in extraordinary detail. The microscope itself is the result of a scientific breakthrough in the study of subatomic particles.

How Organisms Work

Every living thing on Earth is made from cells—individual units that can combine and work together to create incredibly complex systems, including human beings. Biology involves the study of cells, and also the many tissues and organs that go into creating living things.

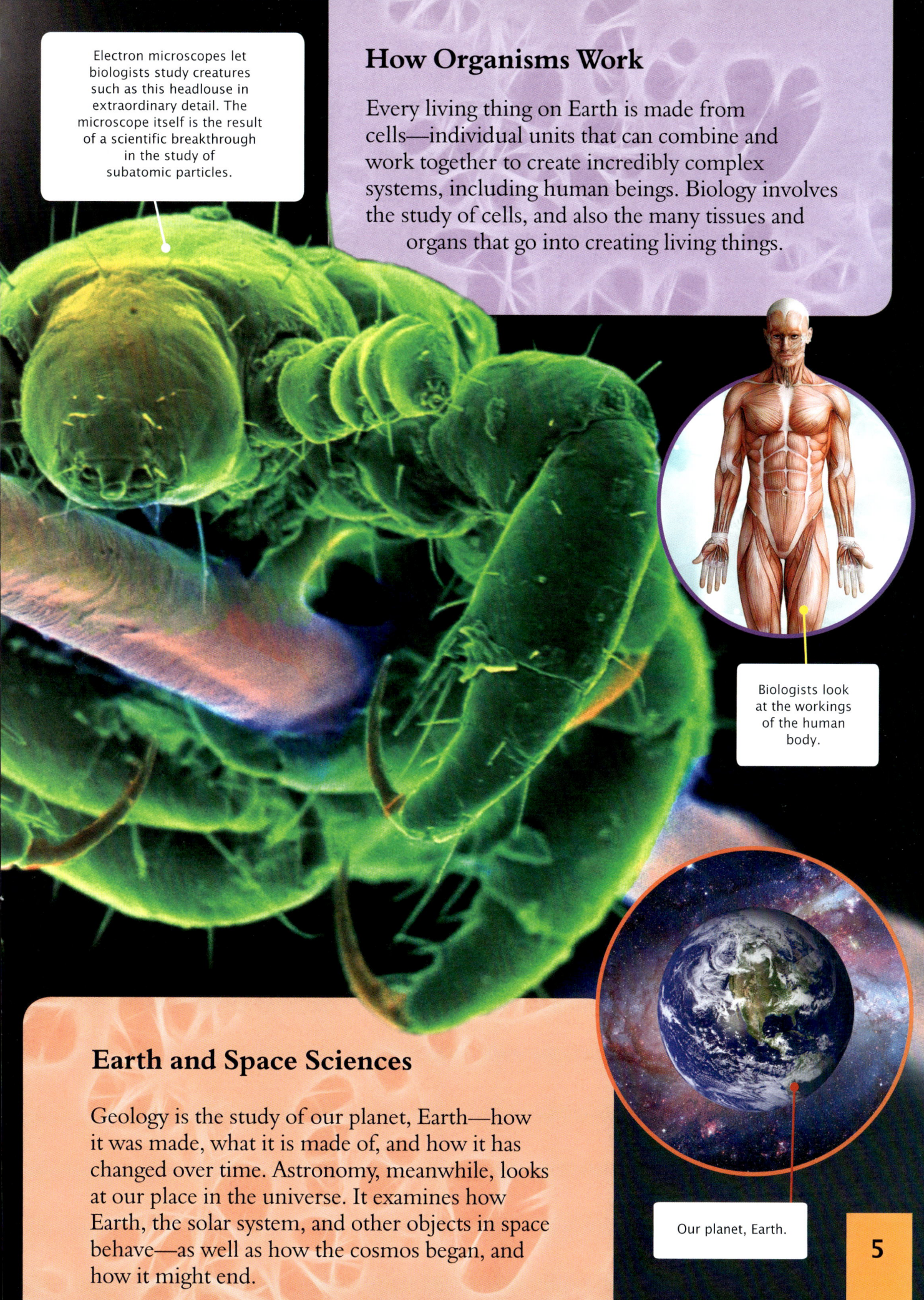

Biologists look at the workings of the human body.

Earth and Space Sciences

Geology is the study of our planet, Earth—how it was made, what it is made of, and how it has changed over time. Astronomy, meanwhile, looks at our place in the universe. It examines how Earth, the solar system, and other objects in space behave—as well as how the cosmos began, and how it might end.

Our planet, Earth.

5

Simple Machines

Ramps, wedges, levers, wheels and axles, screws, and pulleys are all simple machines that people have used since ancient times. Ramps and wedges might not seem like machines, but they are. Machines are devices that use the laws of physics to make tasks easier.

Making Work Easier

Doing any physical task involves work—in other words, applying a force to an object that moves it. The amount of work for a particular job is always the same, but a machine makes it easier. The machine multiplies the amount of force we apply, or it increases the distance over which the force acts.

Even before the invention of the axle, the people who built Stonehenge may have used basic wheels—sledges on rolling logs—to move massive stones.

Simple to Modern

Ancient inventors found many ingenious ways to power their simple machines. They used the weight of falling water, the movement of tides, and the force of wind. Modern machines date from the Industrial Revolution. In 1712, Thomas Newcomen built the first successful steam engine, which used the force of expanding or condensing steam to power machines.

This 1834 engraving shows a textile factory with steam-powered printing machines. Steam was used in industry till the early 1900s, when electricity began to take over.

The farther away the swings are from the axle, the faster they move.

6

The swings are attached to a wheel. The wheel turns when force is applied to the central axle.

A wheel won't work without an axle—a central rod or cylinder that it can turn around. The wheel and axle work together to help things move. The force can be applied to the wheel or the axle.

A motor moves the axle. The circle turned by the wheel is much larger than the circle turned by the axle.

AMAZING DISCOVERY

Scientist: Archimedes
Discovery: Machines of war
Date: 213 BCE
The story: Greek mathematician Archimedes built pulley systems, cranes, catapults, and other machines to help defend his home city against invading Roman ships in 213 BCE. He also wrote the first proper explanations of the science behind such machines.

Engines, Motors, and Generators

Engines are machines that use one form of energy (such as heat or electricity) to produce another—motion energy that can do work. Steam, gas, and diesel engines all burn fuels to create this energy. Electric motors rely on electricity and magnetism.

Electric Motors

An electric motor works because of the relationship between permanent magnets and an electromagnet. A spinning rotor sits in a drum lined with fixed magnets called stators. Alternating current passes through coiled wires around the rotor. It produces a changing magnetic field that pushes the coil away from the stators.

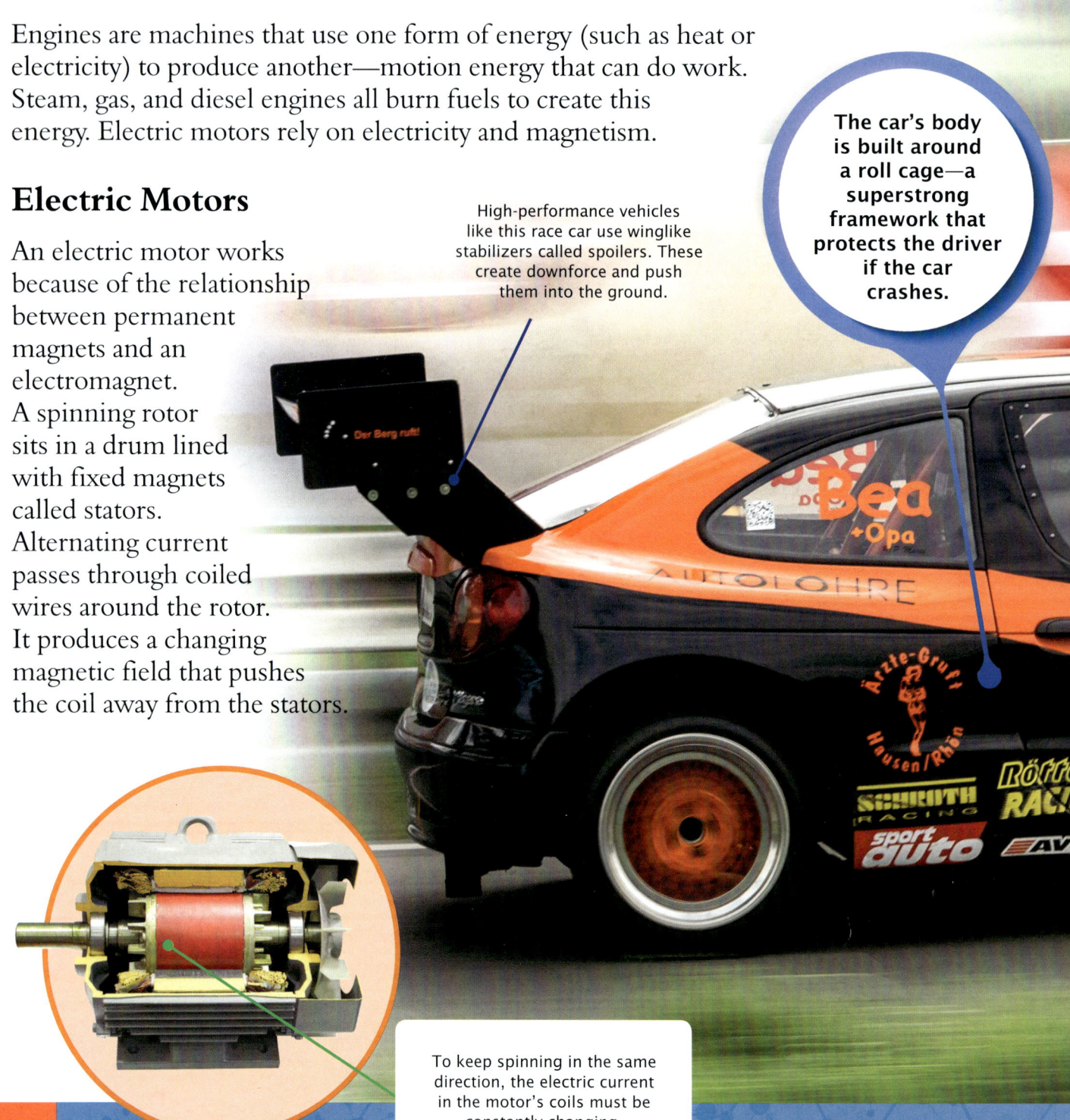

High-performance vehicles like this race car use winglike stabilizers called spoilers. These create downforce and push them into the ground.

The car's body is built around a roll cage—a superstrong framework that protects the driver if the car crashes.

To keep spinning in the same direction, the electric current in the motor's coils must be constantly changing.

AMAZING DISCOVERY

Scientist: Ányos Jedlik
Discovery: Spinning electric motor
Date: 1828
The story: Hungarian scientist Jedlik came up with the key to a working electric motor. He worked out that changing the direction of current flowing inside an an electric coil would keep it spinning in a ring of magnets.

Generating Turbines

Turbines are one of the most common ways of producing electricity. They work like an electric motor in reverse. Motion energy spins a wire-wrapped rotor in a magnetic field and makes current flow in the rotor wires. The motion energy can come from expanding steam, water falling from a dam, ocean waves, or gusts of wind.

This cutaway shows the insides of a wind turbine, which makes "green" or renewable electricity. The motion energy comes from the wind turning the blades.

A combustion engine turns chemical energy (the combustion, or burning, of fuel) into mechanical power.

Most car engines burn gasoline/petrol (ignited by an electric spark) or diesel fuel (ignited by compressed hot air).

9

Electronics

Electronics are built into our televisions, smartphones, games consoles, laptops, and e-books. Everyday appliances such as washing machines and dishwashers rely on them, too. Electronic devices control and adjust the flow of small numbers of electrons in an electric current. They can use the electric current to represent some kind of signal or information.

Electronic Components

The first electronic devices were amplifiers that could boost weak currents to useful levels. These amplifiers were like valves, and made current flow in only one direction. The same technology made radios and computers possible. Today's valves, called diodes and triodes, are incredibly small. They are made using materials called semiconductors.

A CD player's lens directs intense laser light created by a special diode onto the reflecting surface of a CD.

Tiny pits cover the disc. These dots or dashes represent digital information such as games, music, or pictures.

Adding other elements to these thin wafers of silicon will turn them into semiconductors. A semiconductor creates a barrier that lets current flow in only one direction.

AMAZING DISCOVERY

Scientists: John Ambrose Fleming, William Shockley
Discovery: Valves and transistors
Date: 1904, 1947
The story: In 1904 Fleming invented a lightbulb-like device called the valve diode, which caused a strong current to flow one way when a weak current was received. In 1947 Shockley used semiconductor materials to build tiny transistors that did the same thing.

10

CD, DVD, and Blu-Ray players all rely on the same kinds of electronic technology.

Analog and Digital

Analog electronics uses currents that change strength to transmit their signal, but electrical interference can damage the signal. Digital electronics isn't affected by electrical interference. It uses currents with just two possible values (the numbers 1 or 0—also known as "bits"). The system where 1s and 0s can stand for any number is called binary.

The pits reflect the beam in different directions. A light-detector converts the flickering beam into electric current.

The digital electronic display on a car dashboard shows the driver information, such as speed of travel or even navigational maps.

11

Computers

At its most basic, a computer is a device that does simple calculations very quickly, even for very large numbers, and identifies patterns in the numbers. By adding clever design and programing to this basic mathematical ability, we now have computers that can carry out a mind-boggling variety of different tasks.

The Brain

The computer's central processing unit (CPU) "reads" information stored in the computer's memory, performs calculations, and then "writes" results back to other parts of the memory. Electronic components called logic gates let the CPU do mathematics and make decisions based on binary numbers (strings of 1s and 0s).

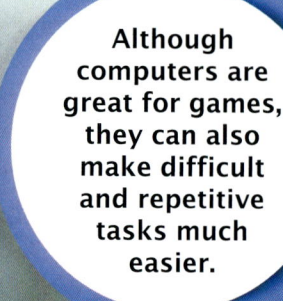

Although computers are great for games, they can also make difficult and repetitive tasks much easier.

Built between 1943 and 1946, room-sized ENIAC was one of the first digital computers. It could carry out 5,000 instructions a second.

AMAZING DISCOVERY

Scientists: Charles Babbage, Ada Lovelace
Discovery: The analytical engine
Date: 1837, 1843
The story: In 1837, long before electronics, English inventor Babbage designed a universal computing machine using brass wheels. It was never built, but mathematician Lovelace worked out the commands needed to run it, making her the first computer programmer. She published her findings in 1843.

Computer Memory

Computers store information they need fast access to on memory chips. Basic operating instructions are written on permanent Read-Only Memory (ROM) chips. Less urgent data, such as applications or the user's files, is saved on a slower magnetic hard disc and then moved to faster Random Access Memory (RAM) chips when it's needed.

Special computer circuits can create sounds from digital files.

A computer's motherboard connects up all of its various components, including the CPU, ROM and RAM memory chips, and hard disc drive.

Special graphics processors (GPUs) create realistic moving images on the screen.

A mouse lets the computer user highlight and manipulate items on the screen.

13

Connected World

Our phones, televisions, Internet, and many other modern technologies rely on computers and other machines being able to talk to each other over huge distances. They communicate by sending their signals through networks of wires or cables or by beaming them through the air in electromagnetic radio waves.

Sending Signals

We send analog signals in two forms. We can use electric current, changing or modulating its strength to transmit the signal; or we can use radio waves, and change their shape. Either way, a receiver decodes the patterns to work out the signal. Today, however, most signals are sent digitally. The information is converted into streams of binary numbers, and sent between machines as 1s and 0s.

Hylas 1, a communications satellite, circles the Earth in the same time it takes Earth to spin on its axis. Its orbit is 22,245 miles (35,800 km) above the equator.

HYLAS 1

Satellites such as *Hylas 1* are solar-powered—they generate their electricity from sunlight.

A phone mast can beam out hundreds of calls at the same time. The signals are digital so they cannot get mixed up like the "crossed wires" of the past.

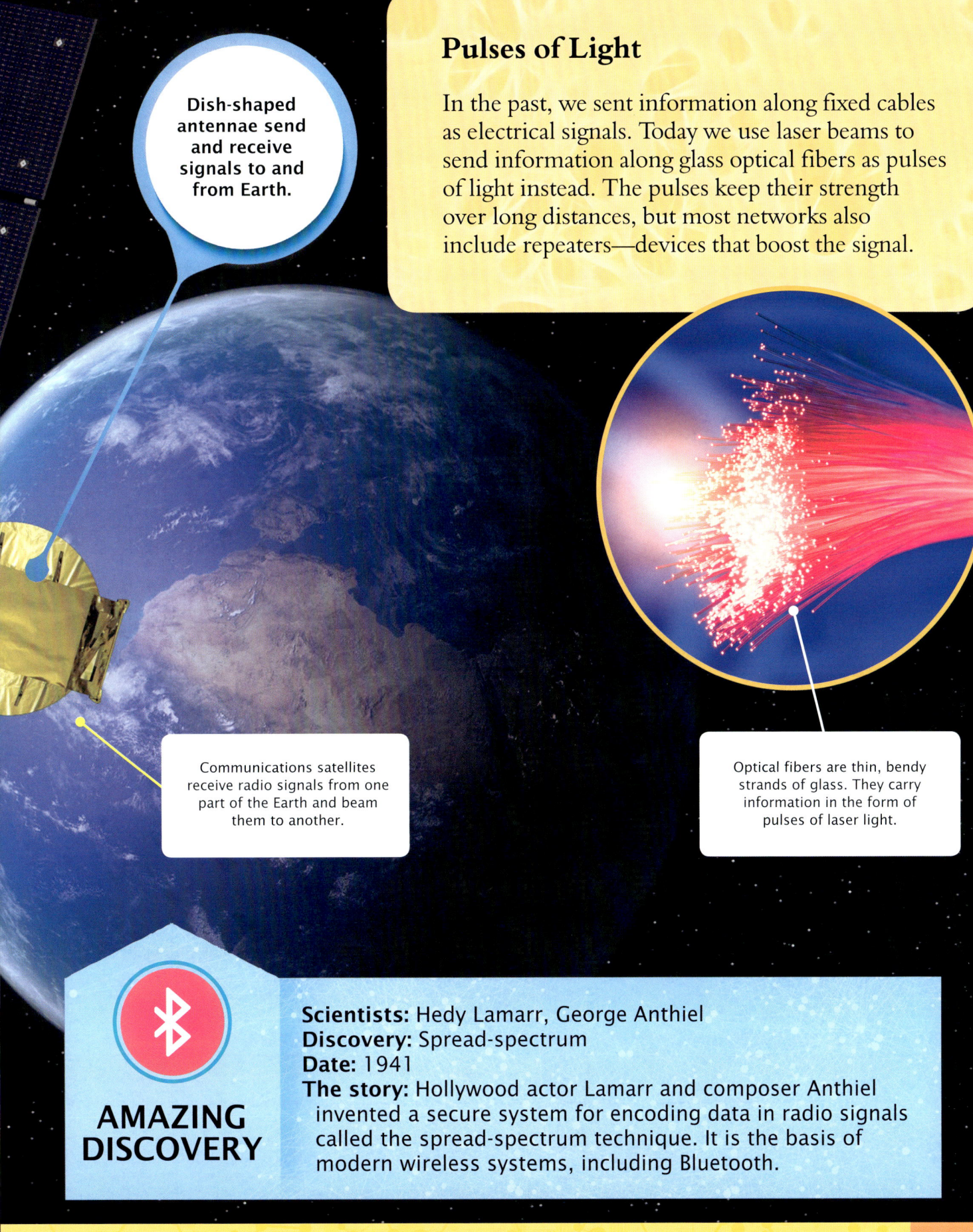

Dish-shaped antennae send and receive signals to and from Earth.

Pulses of Light

In the past, we sent information along fixed cables as electrical signals. Today we use laser beams to send information along glass optical fibers as pulses of light instead. The pulses keep their strength over long distances, but most networks also include repeaters—devices that boost the signal.

Communications satellites receive radio signals from one part of the Earth and beam them to another.

Optical fibers are thin, bendy strands of glass. They carry information in the form of pulses of laser light.

AMAZING DISCOVERY

Scientists: Hedy Lamarr, George Anthiel
Discovery: Spread-spectrum
Date: 1941
The story: Hollywood actor Lamarr and composer Anthiel invented a secure system for encoding data in radio signals called the spread-spectrum technique. It is the basis of modern wireless systems, including Bluetooth.

Flying Machines

Humans have always dreamed of taking to the air. In the 1780s the French Montgolfier brothers became the first to achieve this with their hot-air balloons. However, powered and steerable flight only became possible in the 20th century.

Like a Bird

Powered aircraft have birdlike wings that generate an upward force called lift. The wing's shape creates a difference in the air pressure above and below that pushes it upward. Aircraft wings can't flap like a bird's, so they must move much faster through the air to keep the plane off the ground.

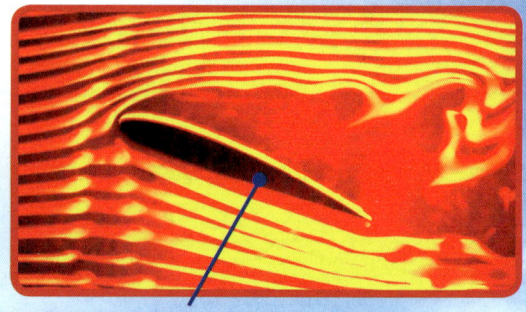

This image of a wing being tested in a wind tunnel shows how air is forced faster over the upper surface. Adjusting the shape and angle of the wing affects the amount of lift.

Up, Up, and Away

Helicopters produce lift with their rotor blades—spinning wings that cut through the air without the entire aircraft needing to move. The fast-moving tail blade generates a sideways force that stops the machine from spinning with its main rotor.

Helicopters can take off and land vertically. The pilot adjusts the angle of each spinning blade to alter the amount of lift it produces, and tilts the entire rotor to push the helicopter forward.

The fuselage (aircraft body) of metal alloys and other materials is both strong and light.

The bullet-shaped nose reduces drag, helping the aircraft cut through the air at high speed.

Jet engines use spinning blades to compress air before using it to burn fuel. Hot exhaust gases blown out of the engines push the aircraft forward.

Flaps on the wings adjust their shape to alter how much lift they create.

AMAZING DISCOVERY

Scientists: Orville and Wilbur Wright
Discovery: Aircraft controls
Date: 1903–1905
The story: The American Wright brothers invented controls that let them control the precise angle of an aircraft in the air, and the shape of its wings. This helped them to make the first powered, controlled flight in 1903.

Smart Materials

Some materials can react to their surroundings in a useful way. Smart materials change when they are exposed to something like temperature, light, pressure, electricity, or a magnetic field. They already have many uses, and they'll become even more common in the future.

These smart glasses are made from a superelastic mix of titanium and metal.

Materials with Memory

Some of the most amazing smart materials are alloys (metal mixtures) and plastics with built-in "memory." They can be crushed or reshaped, but they change back to their original state when they are "told to"—for example, if they are heated or dampened.

NASA scientists hope to build aircraft with smart wings. The idea is that the wings could sense alterations in air pressure and change their shape to suit flying conditions.

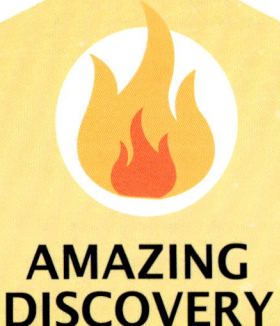

AMAZING DISCOVERY

Scientists: William J. Buehler, David S. Muzzey
Discovery: Nitinol
Date: 1962
The story: Buehler, a researcher at the US Naval Ordinance Laboratory, discovered this nickel-titanium mix. Its smart properties were discovered by chance in a laboratory meeting, when Muzzey held a lighter under a bent sample and found it slowly returned to its original shape.

Smart Power

Photovoltaic (PV) semiconductors (solar panels) are among the smartest materials humans have ever made. They make electricity for us from sunlight. Their atoms lose electrons when they are exposed to photons (light particles)—the electrons flow to an electrode as current. PV materials react to temperature change.

We use PV semiconductors in solar panels for making pollution-free energy on Earth, and for powering satellites and spacecraft.

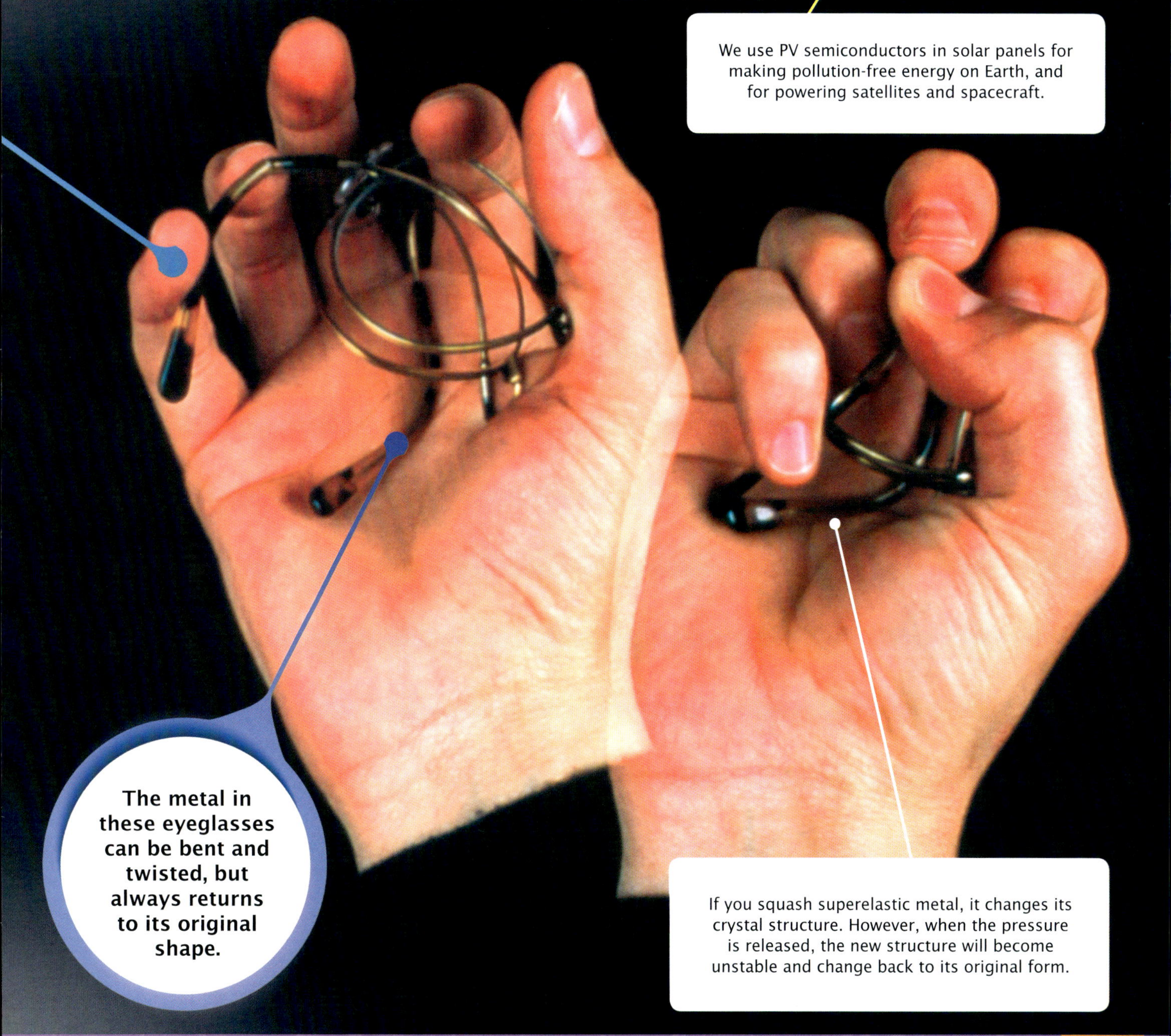

The metal in these eyeglasses can be bent and twisted, but always returns to its original shape.

If you squash superelastic metal, it changes its crystal structure. However, when the pressure is released, the new structure will become unstable and change back to its original form.

Nuclear Energy

Compared to its size, the forces at work inside an atom's central nucleus are enormous. Nuclear power plants tap into this huge energy source. They use a process called nuclear fission that makes some heavy, unstable atoms split into smaller, more stable forms.

Nuclear Fission

Fission happens all the time in nature. Nuclei of elements such as uranium are naturally unstable or "radioactive." They disintegrate at random, releasing small bursts of energy. Nuclear power harnesses this process by creating a chain reaction. Each disintegration instantly triggers several more, and a trickle of energy turns into a torrent.

The US National Ignition Facility (NIF) houses the world's largest, most energetic laser. It hopes to copy the nuclear fusion going on in the Sun to provide an unlimited, cheap source of electricity.

Nuclear power plants use the energy they release to turn water into steam. The steam drives electricity-producing turbines and then escapes through huge cooling towers.

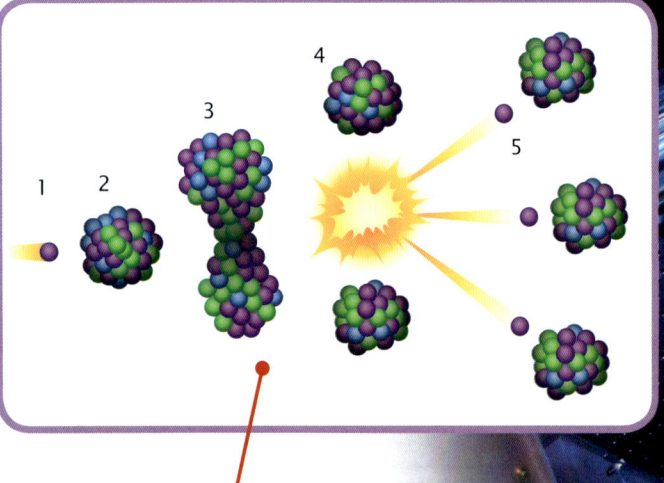

In a fission chain reaction, a neutron particle (1) strikes an unstable atom (2), making it split apart (3). The fission process leaves behind smaller nuclei (4) and more neutrons (5), and so the nuclear reaction can start all over again.

Future Fusion?

Fusion reactions release energy by joining lightweight nuclei instead of breaking apart heavy ones. Unlike fission, fusion does not involve rare heavy elements and doesn't leave behind long-lasting pollution. It sounds like a recipe for cheap, clean energy, but the problem is that fusion only takes place at temperatures like those in the core of the Sun.

The laser beams in the NIF surround a pellet of hydrogen fuel. They compress and heat it to the point where nuclear fusion takes place.

The NIF aims to start a reaction that keeps going on its own—a goal no fusion experiment has yet achieved.

AMAZING DISCOVERY

Scientists: Lise Meitner, Otto Hahn
Discovery: Nuclear fission
Date: 1938
The story: Meitner and Hahn discovered that uranium atoms will decay when struck by smaller neutron particles, releasing energy. Because uranium decay also releases neutrons, it is the key to a nuclear chain reaction.

21

Nanotechnology

Imagine machines made up of individual atoms, able to copy themselves, assemble objects, and even repair our bodies or fight disease at a molecular level. This is the idea behind nanotechnology—and while this new science hasn't yet delivered all these dreams, it is already starting to affect our everyday lives.

Teeny-Tiny Tech

Nanotechnology involves building on the scale of nanometers (billionths of 3.3 ft/1 m) or less. Nanomaterials are substances with engineered atomic-scale structures that give them useful properties. We already use them to make self-cleaning glass, dirt-repellent paints and sprays, and superfine filters for purifying water and trapping viruses.

Carbon nanotubes can be used in touch-screen devices, such as tablets, and high-strength bullet-proof vests.

Building with Atoms

Nanoengineers can also build structures out of individual atoms. They use a machine called an atomic force microscope to "see" the separate atoms on a material—and they can even pick them up and move them around! This technology could eventually let us build complex computers atom by atom.

Scanning tunneling microscopes are the best way of mapping and building with single atoms.

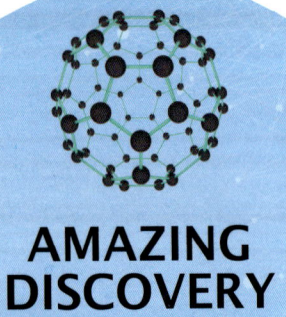

AMAZING DISCOVERY

Scientists: Richard Smalley, Robert Curl, Harold Kroto
Discovery: Fullerenes
Date: 1985
The story: Smalley, Curl, and Kroto led a team of chemists who discovered a ball of carbon atoms that they called buckminsterfullerene. This was the first hint that carbon could create strong rings and tubes for use in nanotechnology.

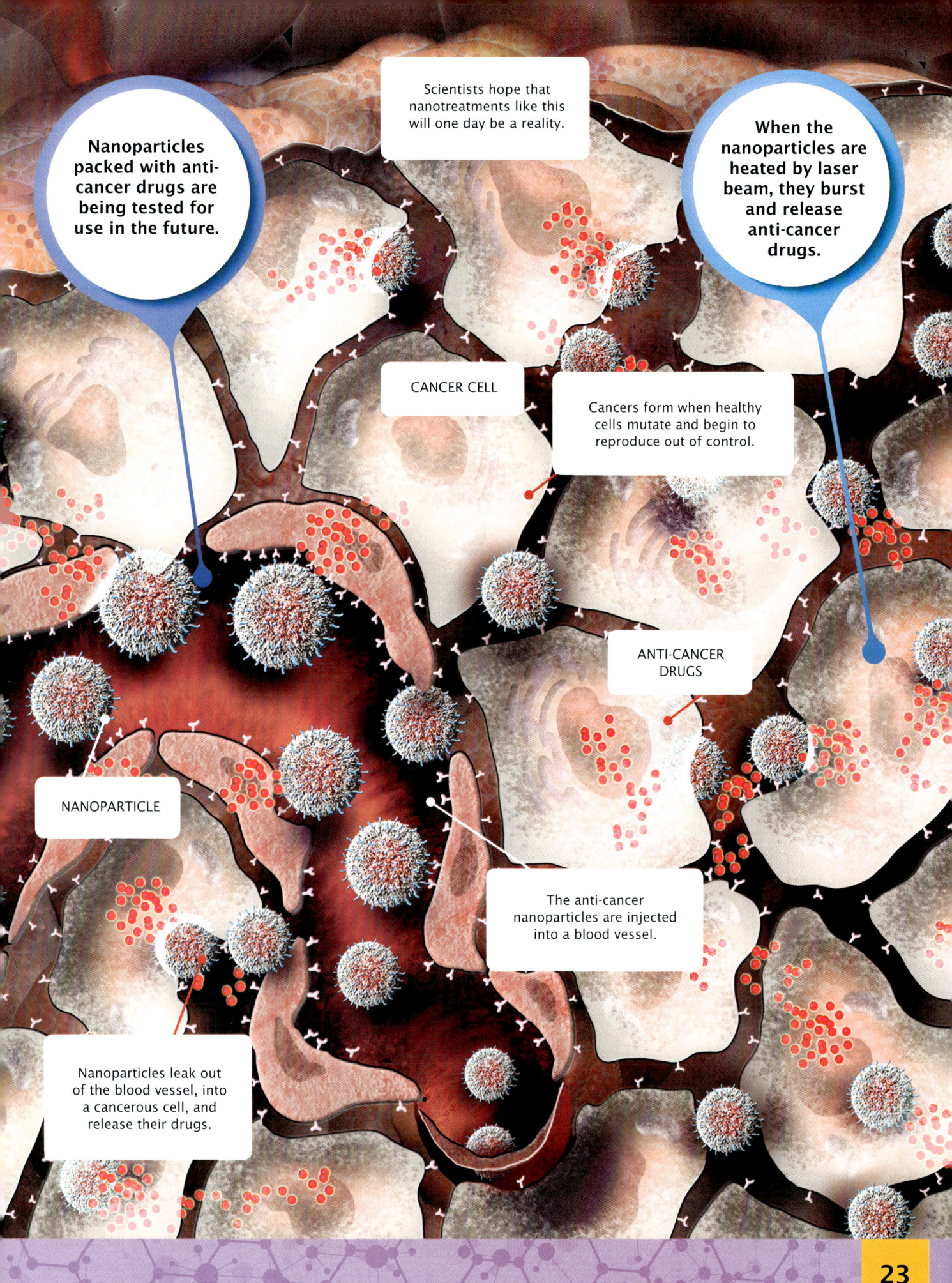

Genetic Engineering

> Crops can be given genes from other organisms which carry benefits, such as resistance to pests or drought.

Genetic engineering lets scientists alter the genes of living things, from plants and animals to human beings. Selecting DNA molecules that carry specific genes can have exciting results, such as preventing diseases. But it also raises a tricky question: will we clone humans? And would the clones be truly human?

Engineering Methods

Simple genetic selection helps to avoid inherited diseases. Doctors fertilize a woman's eggs in a laboratory, check them for the disease-causing gene, then implant disease-free eggs into her uterus. A more complicated technique, known as gene editing, replaces parts of a particular DNA strand that carry faulty genes.

Gene editing involves using a pair of chemical "scissors" to enter the cell and replace the faulty DNA. The corrected DNA strand is then copied each time the cell reproduces.

Cloning

Clones are organisms that have identical genes. Geneticists replace the nucleus of an egg cell with one from a donor individual. The new nucleus divides and reproduces to create stem cells—special cells that can create or repair any kind of body tissue. The resulting clone has all the same genes as the donor.

The first and most famous cloned mammal was a sheep called Dolly. She is shown here with Ian Wilmut, who helped to create her.

Genetically modified (GM) food is allowed in some countries but not in others. Some people have doubts about eating it, but there's no evidence it causes harm.

Scientists must take care that GM crops do not breed with other farmers' normal crops.

AMAZING DISCOVERY

Scientists: Ian Wilmut, Keith Campbell, the Roslin Institute
Discovery: How to clone a mammal
Date: 1996
The story: Wilmut, Campbell, and their team created Dolly by injecting the nucleus of a cell from a Finn-Dorset sheep into an egg cell from a Scottish Blackface. Then they implanted the embryo into a Blackface surrogate mother.

Fun Facts

Now that you have discovered lots about technology, boost your knowledge further with these 10 quick facts!

An axe's wedge-shaped head is a simple machine. Force applied to the thick end becomes concentrated in the thin edge so that it has enough pressure to chop.

The world's tiniest electric motor is just one-36,000th of the width of a human hair. It was built from a single molecule in 2011.

A string of eight bits can represent any number from 0 to 255. 64 bits can represent any number up to 9,223,372,036,854,775,807.

An iPhone X processes 600 billion instructions per second.

Signals have been successfully sent more than 6,214 miles (10,000 km) along optical fibers without using repeaters to boost them.

Russia's Antonov An-225 is the world's biggest aircraft, with a wingspan of 262.5 ft (88.4 m). It can carry up to 550,000 lb (250 tonnes) of cargo.

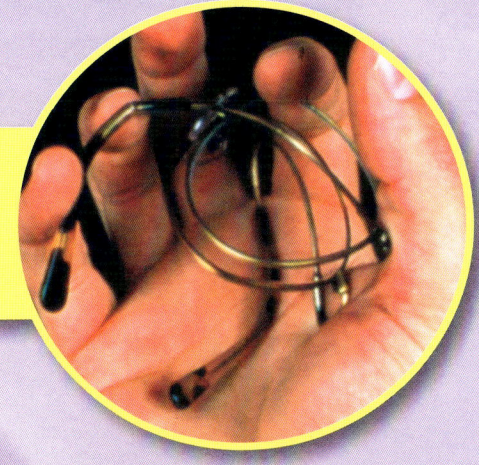

Shape-memory alloys have to be "trained" into their original shape. Nitinol is heated to 932°F (500°C) for 30 minutes, shaped, and then rapidly cooled.

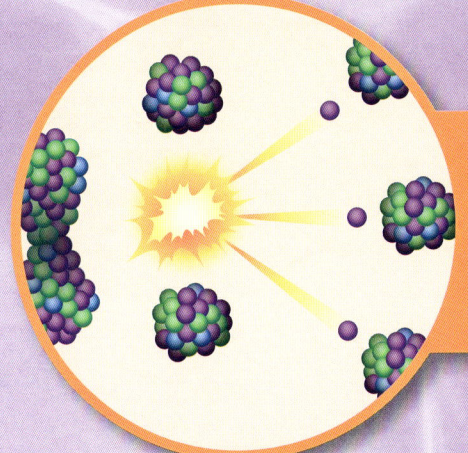

Fission uses rare forms of elements called isotopes. A small sample of the uranium 235 isotope generates 3.7 million times more energy than the same amount of coal.

The nanoengineers who built "geckotape" were inspired by the billions of nanoscale hairs on a gecko's feet. It sticks to any surface using forces between molecules.

In 2012 scientists in Utah used genetic modification to create goats whose milk includes the same proteins as super-strong spider silk.

27

Your Questions Answered

We have developed an incredible amount of technology to help us in everyday life, as well as in many areas of science. But there is always more to discover. Scientists and engineers are still researching and developing new types of technology to help us fight disease, grow more food, and harvest energy in more environmentally friendly ways. Here are some questions about technology that can help you understand more about this vast and fascinating topic.

How do touchscreens work?

The touchscreens we use to operate smartphones are called capacitive touchscreens. They consist of a layer of conductive material, covered by glass, which is insulating. In order to operate the screen, it has to be touched by something conductive, such as skin. Once the skin connects with the glass, it decreases the electrical charge in the conductive layer. The electronics in the phone register the location of the change in charge and pass on to the phone's computer.

Capacitive touchscreens react to touch, rather than pressure.

In the future, will nanoparticles be used in everyday life?

Nanoparticles are already being used in our homes every day! From the kitchen sink and the microwave, to cosmetics and laundry detergent, nanoparticles perform incredibly useful and important tasks in every household. For example, they form antimicrobial coatings that are used on fridge handles, in pet food bowls, and on cutlery. Their use will become even more widespread in future.

Can genetic modification be used to fight disease?

In recent years, genetic modification has contributed in many ways to keeping us healthy. One of the main areas that relies on GM technology is the production of pharmaceuticals. Since the introduction of genetic modification, the production of vaccines has become much safer, cheaper, and more widely available. Other uses of GM in medicine range from modifying insect DNA to prevent the transmission of diseases to changing the DNA in a sick patient's stem cells to help the body recover on its own.

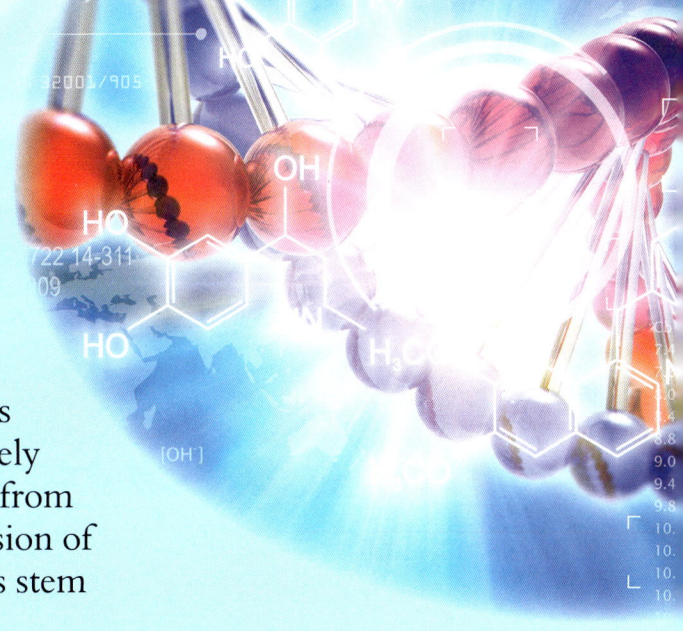

Scientists can use GM to modify a mosquito's DNA, stopping it from transferring malaria to humans.

How do spacecraft fly in space?

Because there is no air in space, the only force a spacecraft is exposed to is the gravity of Earth, if it stays close enough to the planet. If it positions itself in orbit, like the International Space Station, it will remain there without any additional energy needed. When a spacecraft wants to move away from this orbit, all it really needs is thrust. If a spacecraft is heading farther out into our solar system, it may briefly orbit a planet to boost its speed before heading out, in order to save on fuel.

How does GPS work?

Short for Global Positioning System, GPS is used by people around the world to locate where they are, no matter how remote their whereabouts. The system uses over 30 satellites that are constantly orbiting Earth, as well as ground stations, and receivers (for instance in mobile phones). The ground stations constantly locate the satellites, to make sure they are positioned as they should be. The receiver works out the distance between it and at least four of the satellites, and can then tell the user precisely where in the world they are!

GPS satellites orbit Earth along paths that allow at least four to be visible from any point on our planet at any time

Glossary

binary A number system that only uses 1 and 0.

current The flow of electricity.

diode A semiconductor device with two connections.

DNA Short for deoxyribonucleic acid, the chemical ingredient that forms genes. Parents pass on copied parts of their DNA to their children so that some of their traits (like height and hair type) are also passed on.

electromagnet A metal core that is turned magnetic by electricity flowing through a surrounding coil.

electron A negatively charged particle found in all atoms.

Industrial Revolution A rapid development of industry and machinery that started in England in the 18th century.

laser A device that geenrates an intense beam of light.

magnetic field The region around a magnet in which the magnetic force acts.

molecule A group of atoms bonded together to form what is known as a chemical compound. A molecule is the smallest particle that still has all of the chemical properties of a substance.

motherboard The main circuit board in a computer that contains all the important components.

repetitive Something that is characterised by repetition.

rotor The part of a machine that turns, often with blades attached.

semiconductor A device that only allows flow of electricity in one direction.

stator The fixed magnets in an electric motor.

transistor A semiconductor device with three connections.

30

Further Information

BOOKS

DK Publishing. *How To Be Good At Science, Technology, And Engineering.* London, UK: DK Children's, 2018.

Ignotofsky, Rachel. *Women In Science: 50 Fearless Pioneers Who Changed The World.* London, UK: Wren and Rook, 2017.

Levy, Joel. *The Big Book Of Science: Facts, Figures, And Theories To Blow Your Mind.* New York, NY: Chartwell Books, 2018.

Macaulay, David, and Neil Ardley. *The Way Things Work Now.* London, UK: DK Children, 2016.

Richards, Jon, and Ed Simkins. *Infographic How It Works: Today's Technology.* London, UK: Wayland Books, 2016.

WEBSITES

BBC Bitesize Electromagnetism and Magnetism
https://www.bbc.com/education/topics/zrvbkqt
Explore this BBC webpage and find out much more about electromagnetism.

PBS Kids Design Squad
http://pbskids.org/designsquad/parentseducators/resources/index.html?category=technologymaterials
Head to PBS Kids and discover lots of videos and activities to do with technology and materials.

Technology for Kids
http://www.sciencekids.co.nz/technology.html
Visit this website to discover technology activities, videos, quizzes, and much more!

Index

A
aircraft 16–17, 18, 27
Anthiel, George 15
Archimedes 7
analog 11, 14
atom 4, 5, 19, 20, 21, 22
axle 6, 7

B
Babbage, Charles 12
binary 11, 12, 14
Bluetooth 15
Buehler, William J. 18

C
Campbell, Keith 25
clone 24, 25
coil 8, 9
communication 14, 15
Curl, Robert 22
current 8, 9, 10, 11, 14, 19

D
digital 10, 11, 12, 13, 14
diode 10

E
electricity 4, 6, 8, 9, 14, 18, 19, 20
electromagnet 8, 14
electron 10, 19
engine
    combustion 9
    electric 8, 9, 26
    jet 17
    steam 6
engineering 24–25

F
fission (nuclear) 20, 21, 27
Fleming, John Ambrose 10
force 4, 6, 7, 16, 20, 22, 26, 27, 29

G
genetic modification (GM) 24–25, 29

H
Hahn, Otto 21
helicopter 16

I
Industrial Revolution 6
Internet 14

J
Jedlik, Ányos 9

K
Kroto, Harold 22

L
Lamarr, Hedy 15
laser 10, 15, 20, 21, 23
Lovelace, Ada 12

M
magnetism 8
machine 6–7, 8, 10, 12, 14, 16–17, 22, 26
Meitner, Lise 21
memory 12, 13, 18, 27
motherboard 13
Muzzey, David S 18

N
nanoparticle 23, 28
neutron 20, 21

O
optical fibre 15, 26

S
satellite 14, 15, 19, 29
semiconductor 10, 19
Shockley, William 10
signal 10, 11, 14, 15, 26
Smalley, Richard 22
solar panel 19
spread-spectrum 15
stator 8

T
transistor 10
turbine 9, 20

W
wheel 6, 7, 12
Wilmut, Ian 24, 25
Wright brothers 17